A Tender Story of Love and Loss

Peekaboo, Pearly Moon

Written by
Karen DeVries
Illustrated by
Stan Myers

kregel
PUBLICATIONS

Grand Rapids, MI 49501

Peekaboo, Pearly Moon

Text © 2003 by Karen DeVries
Illustrations © 2003 by Stan Myers

Published by Kregel Publications, a division of Kregel, Inc.,
P.O. Box 2607, Grand Rapids, MI 49501.

Library of Congress Cataloging-in-Publication Data

DeVries, Karen
  Peekaboo, Pearly Moon / by Karen DeVries; illustrated by Stan Myers.
      p.   cm.
Summary: A young girl's grandmother teaches her a singing game that her grandmother's father had used to illustrate God's love—a game that helps the girl deal with her grandmother's death.

  [1. Death—Fiction. 2. Grandmothers—Fiction. 3. Moon—Fiction.] I.
Myers, Stan D., ill. II. Title.
  PZ7.D521115 Pe 2003
  [E]—dc21

2003004078

Interior Design: John M. Lucas

ISBN 0-8254-2448-8

Printed in Hong Kong

1 2 3 4 5 / 07 06 05 04 03

The Gift of Heaven

Children have the beautiful ability to process their grief by fully integrating and accepting loss more quickly than adults. They express their feelings repeatedly, but then make a more complete resolution of them and are able to move on. It's important that we provide concrete, honest information about the grieving process, especially when children initiate discussion.

Our children sense our emotions even when we believe we're doing a wonderful job of concealing them. It is healthy for children to see the sadness that accompanies our loss. Moreover, when they see us cry out to God in abject sorrow, then later witness the return of joy to our lives, they gain a respect and understanding of God's redemptive power. They come to know they are permitted to share their hearts openly with our perfect father, God, which brings comfort and growth in their faith.

Facing the death of a loved one offers perhaps the most teachable time to reinforce the assurance and comfort that God will never leave us or forsake us, and that our eternal hope rests in knowing we have the gift of being with him forever in heaven.

We find comfort, hope, and encouragement in the Bible.

Verses about heaven:

Matthew 18:10	John 14:1–2	1 Corinthians 2:9	Revelation 4:2–4, 6
Revelation 5:11, 13	Revelation 7:17	Revelation 21:18–21	Revelation 22:3b–5

Verses that will provide comfort:

Deuteronomy 31:8	Psalm 30:11	Psalm 46:1	Isaiah 41:10
Matthew 5:4	Matthew 11:28–29	2 Corinthians 1:3–4	Philippians 4:4–7

Grandmother's relatives are from Italy.

She likes to tell me stories of her father, a musician, who sang to the moon long ago. Her father's song was a game. A peekaboo game.

Grandma begins to sing her song as the great ball dances behind a moving cloud, then out again.

"Peekaboo, pearly moon," Grandma says, laughing quietly.

My smile joins her soft laughter.

can see how she still loves this funny Great-grandpa I've never met.

"I miss my father," she sighs. "He taught me how life can be like a peekaboo game."

"A peekaboo game?" I ask.

She looks from the sky down to my curious eyes.

"My father told me that God's love is always peeking at me. It's so big that I can't see it all —especially when I let a mad or bad mood, like that big gray cloud, get in between God and me."

I like Grandma's game. I don't like that she's sick. I don't like that I'll miss her so much when she goes to heaven.

We play "Peekaboo, Pearly Moon," and it helps me to not feel so sad.

I sing "peekaboo" as I pass out hugs and kisses good-night. I climb into Daddy's truck for the drive home.

We ride swiftly past the
tall row of golden birch trees.
They turn from gold to silver
in the autumn sky.

"Peekaboo, pearly moon,"
I laugh at the gleaming slivers
of moonlight.

The big red barn with
hand-painted flowers hides
it next.

"Peekaboo, pearly moon,"
I sing as my eyes try to catch
it whole.

The country road winds around the wise, old oak tree. Its swaying branches screen the moon.

I stare up at the strong tree and softly say, "Peekaboo, pearly moon."

I sink into silence as the proud gravestones of Oakwood Cemetery cast shadows in the moon's glow.

"Peekaboo, pearly moon," I whisper.

*W*e whisk by a neat row
of cottages along Silver Lake.
The moon flashes and
vanishes.

"Peekaboo, pearly moon,"
I chant. "Peekaboo, pearly
moon."

The bell tower over Boulder
Creek Church seems to swing
the moon as we cruise past.

"Peekaboo, pearly moon,"
I tease.

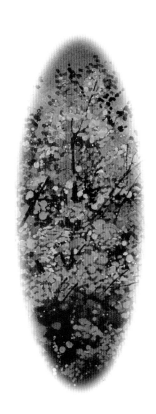

Dad helps me snuggle into my bed. I look out into the moonlit sky. I thank God for the new peekaboo song Grandma has taught me.

"Peekaboo, pearly moon until tomorrow night, when I'll visit my sweet Grandma again," I say before closing my eyes.

Driving back to Grandma's, it is almost dark enough to play "Peekaboo, Pearly Moon."

We pull up to her house. I jump out of Daddy's truck and run to her. She has that far-away look in her eyes when I greet her.

"Grandma, are you thinking about Great-grandpa's 'Peekaboo, Pearly Moon' game?" I ask.

Looking at the moon, Grandma smiles and replies slowly, "I am thinking about the perfect place where Great-grandpa is. I will be going there soon."

"*B*ut you're looking at the moon, Grandma. That's not heaven!"

Grandma explains, "The shining moon reminds me of the light of heaven, where it will never be dark and I will never be afraid. The gates of heaven are made of pearls. Can you see how the moon could be a giant pearly gate of heaven?"

Grandma continues, "Heaven is a beautiful place where I will sing as sweetly as the angels.

"And in heaven, Great-grandpa is loved. I am loved. You are loved."

"*My* father was right about his peekaboo game. God's love has shown me little glimpses of the blessings of heaven all of my life. Now that I will be going there soon, I can see almost *all* of his love, just like we can see that whole, great big pearly moon tonight!"

That was the last time I played "Peekaboo, Pearly Moon" with my Grandma. When she died, it was hard to understand how she could be so happy when I was so sad.

Now when I see the full moon, I remember Grandma in her new world, heaven, and the songs of peace and joy she is singing.

I close my eyes, and I can still see her smile and hear her soft laughter.

I smile and hum, "Peekaboo, pearly moon."

"The twelve gates were twelve pearls, each gate made of a single pearl."

Revelation 21:21

To Michael, whose curiosity and determination inspire my faith;
Katherine, whose joy and compassion bring song to my soul;
and Dale, whose encouragement and unconditional love
provide friendship true enough to point me toward
the hope for my future.
Thank you all.

In loving memory of my mother, Nonne Norma Jean.
May generations, through Christ, also find their way to heaven.